THE BEGINNING OF MY END

THE BEGINNING OF MY END

THE CHUCK

THE BEGINNING OF MY END

iUniverse books may be ordered through booksellers or by contacting:

iUniverse
1663 Liberty Drive
Bloomington, IN 47403
www.iuniverse.com
844-349-9409

ISBN: 978-1-6632-1103-3 (sc)
ISBN: 978-1-6632-1104-0 (e)

Library of Congress Control Number: 2020920190

Print information available on the last page.

iUniverse rev. date: 11/06/2020

THE STORY BEGINS ON a cold windy rainy winter evening. I was sitting in my living room watching the New York Knicks play against the Boston Celtic. The game was in Boston. I was watching it on my Sony 65" high definition smart TV. I was eating a hamburger drinking a Heineken when the doorbell rang. I immediately stroll across the floor to answer the door. I couldn't believe who was at the door. Zoe Brown my first cousin. We hugged each other and she came in. Zoe sat down on the sofa bed and I sat down on the chair bed. The two chair beds are side by side with each other in a semicircle from right to left. I have pictures of six generations directly over my sofa beds. Zoe started talking, I couldn't understand a word she was saying. I was having an out of body experience. My nose started running, eyes puffy and my fingers started to move by itself. Zoe moved a little closer to me and she started her story all over again. She stated that my mother and aunt had just been murdered. (The Beginning of My End) My mother and aunt had just started to renew their friendship after fifteen years. They lived just ten blocks apart and haven't spoken a word to each other until their mother was sick. The sisters started to hang out together, nails, hair, shopping together. They even took trips together. I knew that they were having a great time renewing all their old friendship. The two sisters were inseparable. Who, What, Why? Anyone wants to hurt them. I could not believe my ears. I laughed, cried, and smiled all at the same time. I laugh and smile at all the good times we had together. The special event we shared with my mother, brothers, and aunt. The outing to the pool, playground, and gyms. The many birthday parties. We were all together smiling, hugging, and having a good time. I cried because the good time will never happen again. I look over to Zoe. A few seconds later she got up, gave me a wave and she headed out the door. Meanwhile, I call an old friend Taylor James. Taylor and I went to High school together. We sold drugs together. I began telling her what had happened to my mother and aunt. I also stated that finding the killer or killers were paramount. Taylor assured me that she would do her best. I sat back on my sofa bed and looked up at the ceiling. The room started looking smaller. My head and ears started to Ring. I glance over to the window and watch the window become smaller and smaller. My body experienced a shutdown. I jumped to my feet headed toward the kitchen and made me a cup of tea. Tea Help me to release negative energy. It also helps me think clearly. It was not my first experience with my out-of-body occurrence but each occurrence became longer and more frightening.

Three days had passed now, not a word from Taylor. Where is Taylor? I wanted to call her but I told myself to Wait for her call. Instead, I call my cousin Zoe Brown. Zoe Love to drive and hang out. I dial her number. Zoe answered the phone. I informed her that I was going uptown for a few drinks. She said ok. She also stated that her two brothers were home from school and she would like to bring them over. I said ok. A few hours later we were all together in my living room. Charles, Carrel, Zoe, and I. We are off to a night of fun and Adventure. I started to tell them about a few bars and clubs I used to attend. A place where people come and go, meet and greet, talk about there's a week, lover and friend. We need to keep our eyes and ears open. We are there for one thing. The name of my mother and auntie killer. The night is about to begin. We all headed down the one flight stairs and out of the building. The 1975 black on black Cadillac brougham was shining and ready to roll. We all jumped into the brougham. I start the car and I hollow out uptown here we come. We will be attending bars, nightclubs, house parties. Roger Pub will be our first stop. The Pub where food and music are free and two drinks minimum. We all step outside the brougham and one by one march into the pub. Music was jumping however there were only two or three patrons in the bar. We quickly turned around, gave the barmaids a wave and we headed back out the door. We got together outside and I told them about Pete and Gene places. An after-hour club, A few blocks away. We jumped back into the Cadillac and we headed toward the club. People were standing around clubs like honey bees. Pete and Gene place, Coke and alcohol flow like milk and honey. We pull up In front of the club and we walk in one by one. Zoe headed straight to the back room where pinballs machine and slot machine are the talks of the night. The brothers headed straight to the bar. They order shot Hennessey with twist lemon and ice. I walk in and look around the club. I looked over on the dance floor and I spotted my kids mother dancing on the floor. I stroll over to the bar and order Heineken with twist lemon. I wait for her eyes to catch mine. We both hesitated a second. Mary made the first move. She swishes toward the bar and hollows out what is the up big boy you looking good. I yell back, you look good yourself Ms. Mary. can, I buy you a drink. Ms. Mary hollowed back you know I don't drink. A glass of orange "juices" and a few cherries will be great. I smiled and I ordered the drinks. Ms. Mary restarts the conversation. She's asked what are you doing uptown. You, looking for (Lucky Strike). I smiled but I said nothing. She continues and stated that our two children were doing great and her family was ok. I jumped into the conversation and stated that I am uptown because someone killed my mother and aunt. Mary put both hands over her mouth and a second later her head hit the table. I jump to my feet to comfort her. It seemed like three to five seconds had passed before she lifted her head off the table. She grabbed my hand and we walked toward the bathroom. We stopped for a second and she looked into my eyes. I will never forget her words. (The Beginning of My End)

Smoke, booze, and women filled Gene and Pete's place. Gene and Pete place where everyone, looking for that special someone or something to fill the night. My eyes scan the rooms. I was looking for the two brothers. I was Hoping that brothers aren't mixing it up too much. I found them sitting on the couch between two young women. I wanted to tell them that night lust and booze bring lifetime pain and hell. I smiled and I moved on. I knew the brother didn't want to here's my story. so, I walked toward the door. I open the door. I couldn't believe my eyes. It was my old running buddy from high school. We gave each other a big hug, We looked at one other. It's been over five years since we have seen each other. We pushed our way back into the clubs and we headed towards the bar. He asked me what I was doing uptown. I told him that we came uptown to enjoy the evening. We drank a few Heineken and we talked about the past like it was yesterday. Five hours had passed since we started uptown. We were all having a ball.

How can I turn this around? What must I do? I started to think about Taylor. Taylor home. Taylor dating someone, Taylor some were making love, Taylor looking for killers, or killers. My mind started to race a hundred miles a minute. I was thinking of every bar, club, house, or dance hall she could be in. Meanwhile, John and I took our drink and we headed to the back room where the pinball and slot machines are located. Zoe is having a ball. She is playing three machines at a time. We stayed at a distance and we watched her. We didn't want to interfere with her concentration. All the time we have been up-town. We have not gotten a call from Taylor or found anyone who knows what has happened to my mother or aunt. It's 4 am. Everyone, looking for that special someone or something. I am looking for a place to eat. I hollow out, where are the house parties? Pete hollowed back, the house party three building up the street. On the right-hand side of the street building number 13 apartment number AAA. I let Zoe know it time to pack it up. She stated, Give her a few minutes. I say you have one minute. The brothers came from the front of the clubs to help her to gather her money and belongings. A few minutes later we are all ready and walking toward the door. I reach for the doorknob and I here's a gunshot. I hear more gunshots. I hear sirens and I here's more gunshot. What is going on in the street? We all huddle down on the floor of the club. Gunshot has turned a night of happiness and adventure into a state of horror. Time is standing still as gunshots cut through the night air. What is going on outside? Who has been shot or killed? The shooting has stopped. We all slowly start to stand and we wonder what could be lurking on the other side of the door. I open the door slow and easy. I look outside. I don't see any police cars or ambulance. I step outside the club and people are walking up and down the street everywhere. I look back and ask Zoe and brothers are they up for more adventure. They all smile but mum was the word. We walk briskly up the street looking for Building number 13. We located the number 13 building.

However, before we could enter, We must use the intercom. We find the AAA button and push it. A few seconds later the door bussers ring. We push open the door. We look around the lobby floors but no number AAA on the lobby floor. We head towards the elevator. We open the elevator door and we walk into the elevator. We closed the doors behind us. We here're a tremendous scream. I grab the handle inside the elevator doors. I whole It tight as I can. We look through the glass and we see a man and woman fighting. The woman has a knife in her hand. Blood is all over the left and the right side of the man's shirts. The man knocks the woman to the floor but before he can do anything she is back on feet swinging the knife wildly. Zoe and the brother again are in disbelief and bewilderment. I push a button and we slowly move away from the lobby floor. Breathing hard, mind racing; finally arrived on the party floor. The music was jumping people dancing everywhere. You can smell the food in the hallway. Big May standing at the door. She looks me up and down. She asks, who are you? Where are you from? She looked me up and down again and she said my goodness, It's Lover's boy. I haven't seen you in years. How are you? I said. I am doing fine. We are here for a few dinners. I would like to have a couple of slices of cornbread and a couple of slices of apple pie. We all smile, big May walk us through the house and into the kitchen. Denise was in the kitchen cooking fish, chicken, salmon cake, rice, collar green. She also had coleslaw and potatoes salad. She turned around and smiled at us and asked how many plates to go, sir. I said six plates to go with cornbread, apple pie, and potatoes salad. Denise and Big May just smile. Big May get the plates ready. They fix each of us a small plate to nibble on. The food is very tasty. We gave Big May and Denise a thumb up. The ladies begin Preparing the big plates to go. We started to talk about the shooting and stabbing and what else could be lurking in the street. The brothers stated this is a big change from term paper and assignments. Zoe stated stop crap let get back downtown. The people uptown are like dogs and cats and they don't give a damn if they kill you or me. It is time to go. Big May and Denise are finished with plates. The dinners are ready. We have three bags. Everyone grabs a bag and I will pay the check. The bill was 70 dollars. I gave Denise a hundred dollar bill and blew her a kiss. We all head out the door and down the steps and into the street. The brougham was five cars up the street toward Gene and Pete's place. We all started to walk briskly up the street toward the brougham. Zoe arrived first to brougham. I threw her the key and downtown here we come. Zoe, Eyes are as large as hamburger as she pierced through the windshield, floored the gas pedal. We leave the horror and suspense behind. Will anything else go astray? Will the food taste as good as it did at Big May and Denise place? Zoe didn't look left or right. She keeps her eyes straight ahead and guns the accelerator as fast as the street lights change.

Thirty minutes later we arrived at 12 12 House Street. We grabbed all the food bags and we all headed up the one flight of stairs. We hear music coming from my apartment. The music was mellow and downbeat. Who was in the apartment and how did he or she get in? We march into the apartment one by one. Savannah Mean was sitting at the table with her legs crossed. looking, fine and sexy. She was wearing a lavender suit with a white silk blouse, lavender boots. She also wore a big glossy diamond ring on her fingers. She was sipping Hennessy on rocks. Savannah quickly jumped to her feet as the crew placed the bags on the table. My eyes came directly in line with Savannah's eyes. She shouts, where'd, hell have you been baby? I gave her a hug and kiss and said uptown checking on the kids and talking to Mary. Savannah smiled, said is that your story or is it the one you are sticking with. O and by the way, I received six calls while you were uptown. You have to remember that your friends are my friends too. A half story is like no story at all, When you tell the truth, I won't have to assume or presume anything. I took a step back from Savannah. The air seemed thick and her eyes did say I love you. I want to tell Savannah everything but women are like a policeman. If you tell them a little bit they tell everyone in the community. You will be guilty before the story is out, It's best to keep your mouth closed and let them assume or presume what they want. A few minutes later, The crew seemed to be finished washing up and they began sitting around the tables. I asked Savannah, would you like something to eat. Her eyes said no but I opened a bag and handed her a plate. She said thanks but the car keys would be nice. I need to make a run. I will be back after night brunch. Savannah gave us a half-wave and out the door, she went. We all sat down and began to eat. Savannah wanted to know why we were all up the town. I think she already has the answer but was upset to see Zoe and brothers come in with me at such a late hour. We continued to eat and talk about our uptown adventure. The brothers said that they had a great time and they received a few telephone numbers. Zoe stated that she won 175.00 dollars and that a 500.00 jackpot was on the way. I said everything sounds great. However, we didn't accomplish our missions. We all finished eating. Clean up the table. We found places to sleep. The brother had the couch-bed and I had the chair- bed. Zoe slept in the bed-rooms. I could hear the brother talk about the mall and what stores that the girls hang around. I could also here's Zoe talking on the phone and she was talking about the mall as well. The Malls is a place where you can meet and greet friends, family, and a place where you buy almost anything.

The next day. The brothers were up early ironing their pants and shirts and getting ready for the mall. They saw me turn over and hollow out were the bacon and hot cake. I hollow back, I don't have any hot cake. I do have bacon and eggs. Everything is in the freezer. The Bread is at the top of the Freezer. I knew the brother would eat me out of the house and home so I made a few salmon cakes yesterday afternoon after I called Zoe. She was still asleep while the brothers were eating and making noise. She awoke just before the brothers started to clean up the kitchen. She came out of the room with her tee-shirt and pantie on. I told Zoe to go back into the room and put some clothes on. She stated that she could walk around with her pantie and tee shirt just like we do with our boxer and tee shirt. We all smile but again mum was the word. Zoe hollowed out, I know some food is left. The brothers looked at each other and said you know we fixed you a big plate sis. Zoe smiled and said I know you did. I made up my chair bed and headed to the bathroom. A few minutes later, I am standing over the stove pulling out my salmon cakes. I place the salmon cake into the pan. I turned around and the brothers were standing around me looking hard. I said to them; if you want anything else to eat you have to go to the store. They slowly moved away from the stove and they looked me up and down and said you're wrong. I said nothing, I continued cooking my salmon cake. I finished cooking the salmon cake and before I could take them out of the pan Miss Zoe was standing over the stove in her panties and tee-shirt with her plates ready for some salmon cake. I just looked and said I am glad you are family. We both smiled, sat down. We enjoyed the salmon cakes. We finished eating and I started cleaning up the kitchen. Zoe headed back to the bathrooms, bedroom. The brother headed out the door and up to the mall.

Later, That evening, The crew was all at the mall and I was home alone waiting for Savannah to return my car. It's around 8.30 pm. Taylor is still no call no show. I am very worried about her. I decided to go outside and have a few drinks with my crew. I walked to the corner and the crew was standing in front of (ABC) store. We exchanged greetings and I asked, have any of you seen Savannah or my car. Someone hollowed out that my car had been stolen and someone else hollowed out that Savannah is across the street with the police. I could not believe what I was hearing, Savannah means everything to me. I just bought her a large diamond ring. Savannah has the key to my heart. Who, Why, Anyone wants to hurt her. I started to walk across the street but before I put my foot on the other side of the street. I have flashbacks of the event that has happened in the last couple of weeks. First, I see Zoe telling me that someone killed my mother and aunt. My body started shutting down and I started sweating, breathing hard. Secondly, I see my cousins and I huddling on the floor Pete and Gene place in horror disbelief. Gunshot filled the night air. Lastly, I see a man and woman fighting. I see blood all over the lobby floor. My mind goes blank for a second or two. I place my foot sidewalk on the other side of the street. I began to look around. I see Savannah sitting next to a police car. I move a little closer and I see police tape and I see the outline of a body on the ground. I start to feel sick throughout my body. Savannah gets up and starts to walk toward me. We give each other a hug and a kiss. She then put her finger on my lip. I have a thousand questions but I can say a word. A few seconds later the Police escort Savannah to the police cars. They don't handcuff her but tell her that she must make a statement at the police station. Savannah is off to Precinct. I am left standing there with no girlfriend or car. A few hours have passed, the police are still questioning Savannah at the precinct. I can't believe that she has been in the station for three or four hours and I can't get a word from the police about Savannah or my car. I need to talk to someone. I'm looking through my phone book numbers and cousin Zoe numbers pop up. I push the ringer and Zoe Browns to answer the phone. What up big cousin, You coming upstairs. what up Zoë? You sound very puzzled. I am a little. Looking at your car in front of my building. However, you sound like you are on the other side of town. What the hell is going on big cousin? I couldn't tell Zoe what was going on yet I asked her to keep an eye on my car. She said ok, A few seconds later, I called my brother and my son. I ask my brothers and my son to meet me over at Zoe's house. They said ok. I didn't tell my brother or son what was going on. I did tell them that it was an emergence. They said to give them a half-hour or so. I said ok. I don't know what is Going On but Savannah and her brother need to answer some questions today. I walk back into the police station and I see Savannah handcuffs to a chair. I am speechless. How long can the police hold Savannah? I need to find out and head over to Zoe's place. I walk over to the police receptionist and I ask her how long can Savannah be held before they must charge her. The receptionist stated that they can hold her for 48 hours. After that, She must be charged or they will release her. I said thank you. I headed back out the door. I jumped on the bus and headed off to Zoe's place. I was thinking about what to say to Zoe and my brother and son without being truthful. I guess I will tell them the truth and let the chip fall where they fall. I didn't tell my crew what was going on yet but things started to change very quickly. I am on the bus. I am sitting down. People are playing loud music, people are looking out the window and people are looking you up and down. I can wait to get off this bus. The bus was like a zoo. Everyone was watching each other. I have two stops and I am off the bus. I pulled the cord. My stop is next. I step off the bus and I look around. I seized a deep breath of relief. I called Zoe. I don't need to run into anything that I can avoid. Zoe let me know Savannah, brothers, and lady friend are standing in front of my car and that the car is parked in front of her building. I tell her to stay alert and that I am walking down the street. We end the call. I started walking down the street. I see five people sitting on a porch on the left-hand side of the street. I look a little farther down the street. I see two or three people looking out the window on the right-hand side of the street. I continue walking slowly. I see two men leaning on a car. All of sudden, I see Savannah's brothers and lady-friend standing in front of my car. I pull my hat down over my eyes and pass right by them and Zoe building. I Know need answers but don't know how to approach the situation yet. I have two options. I can run up on Savannah's brother. I can call him Out. Either way, I know I'm in for a fight or shoot out. I start to pick my poison. I think I should run upon him. I have passed by him so, He won't be expecting anything to happen. I made a quick turn and I started walking back in his direction. I am on top of him within three seconds. He started to run. I put a chokehold on him and he is not going anywhere. My brother and son arrived five seconds later. We now have Him in checkmate. We wanted answers. I asked him What are you doing with the car? Why is Savannah in jail? What hell is going on? He looked up at us as those He had seen a ghost. I knew he wasn't going to say a word. I emptied his pockets. I found three thousand six five dollars and my car keys. I took his socks and sneakers off and found another three hundred dollars and a knife. The lady he was with just took off running down the street. We put him in the back seat of my car and drove him back to my place. He didn't try to fight back or talk. We arrived back at my apartment. I have keys to the basement storefront. We drug him down the stairs and into one of the three basement rooms. I went back up-stair and made a phone call and within ten minutes we had three dogs ready to guard him for as long as we needed them. He was not answering any question, In return, food or water was denied. Who will be the last one standing? Savannah and Savannah's brother were not talking. So, my brother, son, and I got together and discussed what we were going to do with him. My son came up with a great idea. We can drive him to Delaware. We put our hands together. We all agreed. Delaware will be our next move with Savannah's brother. We will be up and moving before 5 am. We will have Savannah brothers hogtied in the back of the van. The trip should take ño longer than two and a half hours. My aunt Terry has a small dairy farm in Dover Delaware. We know she will be glad to see us.

Meanwhile, We have Savannah, brother's secured in the basement. I headed over to the jail. To see, If I can help Savannah? I entered the station and I talked to the desk Sargent's. He informed me that Miss Savannah has already been released from jail. I decided to head back home. A few minutes later I arrived home. I headed down-stairs to check on Savannah brothers again. I get to the door and all seem secure. I turn around and I head back up-stair to my apartment. I opened the up-stair door and music seemed to be coming from someone's apartment. It's early morning and we only have eight apartments in the building. They are playing my favorite song (Stay in my corner by Dell). I get closer to my door and it seems to be coming from my apartment. Who could be in my apartment? I opened the door and I froze in my tracks. Sitting table looking sexy and beautiful Savannah Means. She was wearing a long red dress with long two inches red boots. I walked 0ver to her and put my arm around her and she put her arm around me. I could wait for the bedroom. I wanted Savannah now. I took off my shirt and paint and she took off her dress, boots, panty, and bras. We start making love in the chair. Sweat was pouring from our faces and body. (Stay in my Corner) still playing in the background. I picked Savannah up and we moved to the bedroom where we continue our early day of lust and passion. Evening, We relax, ate a few bowls of fruit and we ordered diners in. We watched a few movies. The next day, I am up early to drive Savannah's brother to Delaware. He has murder robbed and assaulted people for over twenty years his rain of terror stop today. I left Savannah a note with my itinerary for the day. I also left her a few dollars for hair, nail, feet, and an outfit. I head out the door and down the stairs to see what is moving in the street. The Street is clear and nothing seems to be moving. I head back in the building and down the basement stairs to get Savannah, brother. I open the door and I don't hear the dog barking. I become a little alarmed. I peak insides and I see my brother and son standing there playing with the dogs and they are ready to go. I tell my sons, you go up- stair and look up and down the street. I want you to check for the movement of cars and people. You text us when all is clear. Also, take the truck key along with you. We are putting Savannah's brother in the back of the truck. My son runs up the stairs.

A few minutes later he texts all-clear signals over my phone. My brother and I grab Savannah's brother's drag him up the stairs into the back truck within two minutes. If you are wondering why we never used Savannah brothers names is because his name will make you tremble (Chris Cross)

Meanwhile, The two hours Ride to Delaware was long and few words passed back and forth. We Listened to little jazz, oldies, blues, and hip hop. I knew what I was going to do to Savannah's brother but my brother and son had no idea. After, Two hours and ten minutes we arrived in Delaware. We stop at Harbor House and we pick up a few toiletries, beer, and pancake syrup. Seventeen minutes later we are pulling into Aunt Terry Dairy farm. Aunt Terry came out to greet us. Old frail Aunt Terry Moving around like she is twenty years young. She gave everyone a hug and a kiss. We walked into Aunt Terry's house. She already had breakfast prepared. A breakfast fit for a king. We had[Eggs biscuit, ham, hotcake, link sausages, grits, milk, orange juice, cranberry juice, butter pecan ice cream, grapes]. The table looked like it was set for ten people. Every item was in a dish or bowl. A spoon or fork in each bowl or dish. A platter was placed on top of each placemat. This is Southern hospitality at its finest. We washed our hands and face and one by one took our place at the table. I said the grace. A few seconds later we began to eat. We were eating and smiling, not a word was passed across the table. I looked over Aunt Terry. She was watching the morning news. I caught myself and asked to be excused from the table. Southern hospitality and good food have blinded me from my mission. I opened the door and walked to the truck. I open the truck door and pull out a jar of syrup. I then walk around the house. I was looking for an area to place Savannah brothers. I didn't see an area where I could place him. So, I hurried back into the house and I took my seat at the table. My son's hollow out, auntie is there any pear or apple trees on the property. She hollow back stated that there was one of each down by the lake. The trees are located on the south side of the property. She continues saying I don't think anyone goes down there anymore. Wild animals run the area. I haven't been down there in years. We finished eating and we cleared the dishes from the table. We asked auntie could we look around the property. She said yes and we moved outside. We picked up a few sticks and we walked towards the south end of the property. It was some thick brush but we pushed straight thoughts to the lake. Ten minutes later, we are standing in front of the lake. It looks more like a small pond or manmade lake. I looked on the other side of the lake and saw the apple and pear trees. This will be a great place for Savannah's brother's last stand. We continue to look around. It's more than two or three apple and pear trees. It looked more like five or six trees. We walked to the other side lake to see how many trees there were. It was three pear trees and four apple trees. Apples and pears were on the ground everywhere. I said to myself this is the perfect place. So, I said to my brother and son let walk to the east side of the property. We started walking. I pull out my lighter and lits the end of my sticks. I passed it on to my son. I took his sticks and I lit it. I passed my son sticks over to my brother. I took my brother's sticks and I lit it. I keep the last walking stick for myself. I lit the sticks. We continue moving slowly through the trees and bushes. The sound seems to be getting closer and closer. We look at each other with our eyes wide open. I pull out my 45 Smith western. We took a few more steps and wild hogs are all around us but with the fire in our hands, they don't make any advancement. We took a few more steps and they scattered all over the place. We turn quickly around and head back toward my aunt's house. We don't see the house but we saw the path we made when we made our way toward the lake. The smoke, fire, and the trees all seem strange to us but it keeps us safe from the wild animals. We see our auntie house but before we get out of the bushes and trees. We encounter another pack of wild hogs running straight in our path. We stopped for a few minutes to let them pass. We scurry out the brushes and the trees as fast as our legs could carry us. The encounter with wild hogs was more frightening than a shootout on a city street. It left us speechless, bewildered, and glad all in one We were speechless because we could not communicate with each other. We were bewildered because we didn't know if we were going to make it out alive. O, how glad we were to see our aunt House and the opening between the brushes and the trees.

We are sitting in Aunt Terry's kitchen sipping on lemonade and eating left-over from breakfast. I am thinking how in the world we are going to get Savannah, brother, down to the lake. I got up and walked over to Aunt Terry. She was watching TV. I asked Auntie Terry. If roads are leading down to the lake. She smiled then got up and walked over to the window. She pointed to the road twenty yards away from the house west side of the house. We miss the road because we walk east, south. My brother and I walked outside to check on the road. We found the road. I ran back to the truck and I jumped into the truck and headed back to where I left my brothers. He jumped in and we headed towards the lake. Five minutes later we pull up to the lake. I told my brother to stay in the truck and keep the truck running. I jump out and walk to the back of the truck. I opened the doors. The stench was so strong I took my handkerchief out and I tied it around my head covering my nose and mouth. I grab Savannah's brother and drag him out of the truck with every inch of muscle and strength I had. I drug him over to the tree and tried his hands behind the back of the tree. I tried his feet together. I placed tape over his eyes. I opened a bottle of syrups. I pouted the syrups over his head and face. I open another bottle and pour it on his crouched area and around his feet. I took the two empty bottles and I filled them with water and I let them sink to the bottom of the lake. I jumped back in the truck and headed back to my aunt's house. It was 10.45, We arrived back at Aunt Terry's house. My son jumped out of the trucks. He started doing a little landscaping. My brother and I jump out of the truck and started helping him. I pulled out the water hose and I started watering the plants. My brother started the lawnmower and he started cutting the grass. We were moving around just as nothing took place stopping only for water or beer. I wanted to finish cleaning the exterior of the house. Check back on Savannah's brother and I would like to pick up a few bags of apples and pears. I would start heading back to the city. We finished the yard and started working on the house. My son and brother started with the window. They sprayed and wiped down the windows. I started cutting and pruning all the vine that had grown on the house. It was a nail-biting job but after an hour and a half, we finished and started cooling down on the front porch with a little beer and music. It was early afternoon. I said let's head back to the lake. I want to pick up some apples and pears for auntie and ourselves. It seemed like a good idea but will we encounter another wild hogs stare down or even attack. We talked about the situation for twenty-five minutes. My son stated that he was not going under any condition. My brother stated that he was not interested either. nevertheless, I convinced them that the mission was not over and we needed to do one or two more steps to finish the mission. We all looked at each other but no one smiled this time. We all got up and started looking for wood to burn and walking sticks. We throw the wood in the back of the truck and we keep the walking stick up in the front cab with us. I checked my 45 and I put a bullet in the chamber. I also check my two 45 clips making sure that nine rounds are in the clips. My son and brother are sharpening the three machetes that were found in the barn. The trip to the lake is finally about to begin. We are all in the truck. My brother is driving. I am in the passenger seat. My son is in the middle. We are ready for any kind of danger. We arrived at the lake. We get out of the trucks. I tell my son and brother the mission again. First, place all pieces of wood in a semicircle where our back face towards the truck. This way, You can turn and sprint back to the truck easily. Leaves, Passenger door, and driver door open. Secondly, Lite all pieces of wood. Lastly, keep moving, side to side, and up and down this movement will help release some of the fear and tension. Keep your eyes and ears open for any sound other than the truck. We began placing the wood in a semicircle in the rear of the truck. The Truck is facing away from the lake. We all began lighting the woods. Next, We began bagging the apple and the pears. I get half a bag full of apples and pears. I tell my brother and son that I am walking over to the spot where Savannah brothers are tied up. He at the end apple trees about ten yards in past first row bushes. I get there. I find Savannah's brother is gone but the rope holding him to the tree is still tied around the tree. I don't know what to do or say but I know It is time to get the hell away from the lake. I sprint back to where my brother and son are and tell them It's time to go. Grab what you can and let go. We jumped in the truck as fast as we could. I looked up and I forgot the wood that was burning. I told my brother and son that I was going back outside of trucks to throw all the lits piece of wood into the lake. It took about fifteen seconds to throw the wood in the lake. But It seems like two minutes. I came back to the truck safely, breathing hard and sweating profusely. My shirts, pants, and socks were soaked beyond belief. My mind was racing. What has happened to Savannah's brother in five hours? My son and brother looked at me and without saying a word I knew what they were thinking. I started slowly but the words didn't describe completely what was going on. I restarted and stated that Savannah's brother is no longer tied to the tree and his body is not where I left it. There are so many more questions but I don't know where to start. Stung, and Shock, my brother, and son look at me again. Faces scowl with mistrust, disbelief. How can we ever trust you again? Will everything you did today return and bring havoc in our lives. We need to get back to the city as fast as we can. I am once again left to ponder my action.

Later. We are back at Aunt Terry bringing in the apple and pear and packing our bags for our departure. Our hug and kisses will follow along with hope to see you soon. We are on our way back to the city. No regret, remorse, or remembrances, what was said or done. We are an hour away from the city. I get three text messages. One from Mary and one from Savannah last one from Taylor James. Mary, message read (I hope you are having a good day) (I enjoy seeing you.) (You are in my prayers). Savannah, the message read, (baby, I am waiting on you). Taylor, message read (hi this is not Taylor but her baby sister Nina) My sister was killed a week ago and we have since buried her. We have found out that she was shot by women riding in black brougham shining bright. If you have anything to add please call me on her phone. It will be on for another three months. I am very angry because deception has followed me home. It has touched me every way you can imagine. I have deceived my son and brother and lied to my aunt and cousin now, I am going back home to a woman who might be a double or triple murder. We pulled into the truck rental place. I got out and waved to my brother and son and they gave no response verbal or hand. I walk slowly to the bus stop with my head down rejected and confused. A few minutes later I am on the bus. I am thinking, will I be the next victim, will someone be waiting for me around the corner or in the dark? The devil has taken over my mind and body. I am a murder just like Savannah. I know I am down and at the bottoms of the pit but where do I go from here. Will, I drink myself to death. Or, will I turn this around and everything I touch and see turns bright and shiny. A few more stops and I am off the bus. I pull the cord and the next stop is mine. I stepped off the bus and I wished the bus driver a happy evening. I look straight ahead and say to myself, I am coming out of this pit shiny, dancing, and singing. I am ready for Savannah and anything wicked thing she has going on. I am not stooping low ever again in this life. I am walking down the street with my chest out and my head up. A few more streets over and I am home. I see ABC stores and a few of my crew standing in front but I am not stopping. I wavy and keep on moving. A few more doors down and I am home. I walk into the building and no loud music is coming-out from my apartment. I used my key to open up the door. Savannah is there watching television in her bars and pantie and sipping on Hennessey on the rocks. She doesn't get up so I walk over and kiss her on the cheek. I continued to the bedroom where I put my bag down. I took off my clothes and headed to the shower. I am into the shower washing when the shower curtain opens up and in step Miss Savannah. My heart started to beat a little faster and faster. Savannah put her tongue in my mouth. I grab one leg. I grab the other legs. We start making love. Soap all over my body. Water running down my face. Savannah and I holding each other tight. I am in soul heaven. We are holding, squeezing and sweating, and breathing hard for about eight long minutes. We finished up and dried each other off. She slips on one of my large tee shirts. I put on my bathrobe. We headed into the living room where we began to watch an episode of Sanford and Son. Savannah's head hit the pillow. She was out by the time her head hit the pillows. I started looking around the house. Where could she hide a gun? I couldn't find the stash. I looked and I looked. I went and laid down next to Savannah. I wanted to make love one more time but finding that stash was paramount. While watching another episode of Sanford and Son. I started falling asleep but when I saw character Sanford carrying a briefcase my gut feeling said to check the closet. Wherein, the closet could the stash be. I slowly ease myself off the sofa bed and I headed straight to the bedroom closet.

I opened the closet door and stood there looking for about three minutes. I thinking, Savannah put something in her belonging or my belonging. I looked first at the two suitcases sitting in front of closets when I opened the doors. The two suitcases were quarter zip up means that suitcases are empty. I pull them out of the closet. I walked back into the living room and I checked on Savannah. She was still asleep. I went back into the bedrooms and I pulled 1 more suitcase out of the closets. The bags had dust on them. The bags had been in the closet for six months to a year. I knew what should be in each bag but the bags were a lot heavier than I expected. Could this be Miss Savannah's stash? I wanted to dance. Instead, I did a few pushups. I wanted to yell as loud as I could but I restrained myself. I opened the first suitcases. The bag contained three guns, fifty dollars my family picture. The second bag had pictures of a crime scene. I couldn't make out the pictures. I needed a brighter light to check the background. The last bag contains two more guns and an unopened letter. I closed all the bags and put them back in the closet. I return to the living room to check on Savannah. I could not tell if she was asleep or playing possum. I sat on the chair bed and I watched her before falling asleep myself. The next morning Savannah was up washed, dressed, and on her out the door before I opened my eyes. All I heard was the door closing. An hour later, I got up and checked the closet. Two guns were missing and Miss Savannah was gone. I wash- up and I put on some clean cloth and I made a few phone calls. I called my mechanic and I asked him if he had a car that I could use for a week or so. I told him I need it today and within the next hours. He stated that he has a small car that I can use for as long as I need it. He also stated he will be bringing it over within the hour. He hung up. I began my second called. I hear a knock at the door. I jump to my feet and I stroll across the floor. I opened the door and Miss Mary was standing there looking chocolate and fine. She was wearing a long black coat with a fur color. Her pants and boots were also black. She pushed me back into the apartment and closed the door. I stated that I was going to call her. But I haven't found time to call. Mary in return stated, I am not here for that, but to let you know what talk on the street is. Your girlfriend and another girl were shooting at each other. The shooting occurred at the same time we were in the club. You need to get your shit together because I don't want that bitch around my children. I hope you understand. Miss Mary hugged me and stated if you want any of this, she needs to be kicked to the curb. I moved my head upwards and downward motions. Miss Mary turned and headed out the door. Silence, and angry, I sat in my apartment looking and thinking which way to turn. My mother and Aunt and best friend are all dead and I can't find out who the killers Are. Evil lurking behind every door. Is it one of my crew members? Strangers trying to take over (BABY BOY ENTERPRISE). Maybe, It could be my girlfriend, Savannah Mean. Only the story will tell.

I started packing a few personal things and I hauled them down to the basement. I needed to get away from Savannah for a while. Tony, my mechanic should be bringing over the car in a few minutes. Tony arrived and I asked him, could you give me a hand with a few bags. He said yes. We head down to the basements to pick up the three suit-cases and four boxes. We were able to put everything in the trunk of the car. Tony and I talked for a few minutes and he confirmed all the brothers at the shop doing great. Bo, Mike, Fig, and Stacy and Rob were working hard. I gave Tony the hi sign and I add that I will be calling him in a few days.

I'm on the Eastside of town. I took out my phone and started calling around rooms to rent. The rooms were Just as expenses as an apartment on the west side of town. I knew room hunting would be hard but I had no idea it would be this hard. An hour had passed by. Another hour. I was getting mad and tired as hell. The prices kept going up and up for a room. I was on my ten calls.A gentlemen's answers the phone and stated that he had a room with a private bathroom and fully furnished and the price was under eight hundred dollars. I took down the address. I told him a little about myself. I stated that I was 6 2" 220 with dark completion and that my job title was a social worker. I help young and old people on path rightness and self-worth. He seems to like what he was hearing and stated that he will be home for the next hour or so. After that, he will be headed out to the gym for a short workout. I let him know that I was fifteen minutes away but I was only five minutes away. I rush over 432 Len Street and jump from the car and ran up one flight of stairs to apartment #5. I rang the bussers. A big man 6' 5"250 answers the door. I gave him my name and he asked me in. We walked to the room he was renting. The door is open. He walked in and I walked behind him. The room is 25 by 25 with a king-size bed, dresser, A mirror the length of the bed. A floor lamp extended over the bed and a bathroom, walk-in closet. I asked him right away what he was asking for the rooms. He stated 750 month and one-month security. I ask if anyone else is expected today. He looked around the room, He then said no. I pulled out my blue checkbook and wrote him two checks for 750 dollars apiece. I told him he can call the bank. I bring up my things now. He said ok and the door will be open and the key will be on the bed. I headed out the door and I descended stairs but before I took two steps down someone called out to me and said (get your butt back to the west -side). I continue downstairs but before I hit the last step the words hit me again. I was a little spook but I was not frightened. I told myself ok but I continued to my car to retrieve my thing out the car. Voice can't stop me now. I have peace of mind. I am back up in my room placing my things around the room. I opened the closets and I found a 15 on television sitting on the floor. I pick the television up and place it on the top of the dresser and plug it in. It was time for the early evening news. I continue placing my thing around the room and into the closet. All of sudden, I hear a special bulletin on the television. Two people shot and one wounded at Third Street and king. I stay just around the corner from there. I stay at Seconds Street and King. The Police believe the gunman was a woman or someone dressed as a woman. My heart skipped a beat and Savannah, name races throw my mind. I finish up placing my thing around and then fold the used boxes. I lock my room door and I head downstairs to my car. I am in my car thinking about what should I do next. I am sitting there for a few minutes and all of a sudden I bolt from the car and head back up to my room again. I retrieved the suitcases. The suitcases that Savannah placed the guns into and I head back to my car. I start the car up and head back to the west side of town. It took me eleven minutes to get back to Seconds Streets and King and make the turn into my block. I made the turn. I see fifteen to twenty people standing on the steps of the building adjacent to mine. I looked into the crowd as I passed but I couldn't seem to see anyone I knew. I didn't park in front of my building but I parked a few doors down the street. I park the car and then retrieve the suitcase on the back seat of the car. I walk toward my building with a big smile on my faces. I head up the few steps and open the main door. I Step in, closed the door behind me, and headed up the one flight of stairs to my apartment. I open the door and head directly to my bedroom where I open the closet door and place the suitcase back into the closet. I head back out the bedroom, into the living room, and finally into the kitchens. I place my foot in the kitchen and Savannah is standing before me. I was shocked to see her in the kitchen but I put my game face on. I opened the conversation by asking her how was your day. She looks up long enough to say, same as usual. Her eyes were as red as ketchup and her words were as smooth as silk. I continue by asking her did you hear that two people were shot over on the third street an hour ago. Savannah stated quickly you're not the police. I lowered my voice. I asked Savannah, You like to take a trip with me away from the City for a week or two. She looked at me and leaned back in her chair and she said ready to go this weekend. I said not this weekend but let plan for two weeks from today. We can buy a few outfits and we go and have a ball. you all in. She said yes. (The beginning of my end).

The next day Savannah left for work or whatever activities she was into. I pulled out my paper and pen and started writing down things I needed to upgrade our wardrobe and my new room. First I wanted a new cd player. A player that can play over three cd at a time record and remote capability. I wanted to hear and feel the base throw my chair and couch. I would like to here's the base bounce off the walls of my room. I decided to look on the Internet. I went to Google, Bing, Amazon, eBay and I tried Craig- list. I was looking for that special unit and that special sound. I couldn't find my unit on the internet. I showered, shaved, and put my clothes on and I splash on a little brut cologne. I headed out the door to the shops that sell music and music equipment and Best Buy will be my first stop. I looked around the store and I talked to a few sales reps but I couldn't find what I was looking for. I exit the store and check my phone messages. I got back in my car and started to think about a place where they sell everything and the Pawn Shop smack me in the face. The Pawnshops were all over the city but the one with the best deals and the bargaining power was in my neighborhood. I headed over to the store immediately. I pulled up about five minutes later and headed straight in to see and talk to the sale- Rep. I told her what I was looking for. She stated to me that she believes she has what I am looking for in the back room and will be right back a few minutes. The sale-Rep returns with nothing in her hand. She stated that it has been sold early today. I know where you can get a new unit in a day or two. I said yes and she wrote it down for me. I thank her and walk out of the store and to my car. I got in my car and I opened the note. I couldn't believe what she had written down. Amazons.com is where you'd find what you are looking for. The Bose waves Multi cd changers I smile clap my hands together.

I am headed to Tony, Used Cars, and Body- workshop. The texts I received from Nina on my way back from Aunt Terry made me change the colors of the car. I knew something terrible had happened in my car. I am not going to take the blame. So, I took the car over to Tony's body shops. The crew has been working on my Cadillac Brougham for a few days. It's being repainted and the interior is being reupholstered. I am wondering how much work is still needed and how much has been done. I am in the shop. I start looking for my car. I don't seem to see it. I see the fellow and give them a wave and I head straight to the tony office. I am in the office and he is busy approving orders and taking orders. He looked up and said have a seat. I will be with you shortly. He finished up what he was working on and he came around the desk and said your car should be ready. We have been working on the car day and night and the crew loves the overtime and love to see smiles on customer's faces. Ready, you and I can take a look at the car and we find out what else needs to be done. The car is outside in the back of the shop. We walk to the back of the shop but I don't see a door. I only see windows. Tony is standing in front of the window. He pulls down a lever and the door opens. We walk out to the back area of the shop and the Brougham is sitting there looking super sharp. I felt the side, hood, and top of the car. The car felt smooth as silk. The all-white exterior and half whitewall tires made the car stand out. The interior of the car white with black trimming and a moon- roof gave the car the look I was looking for. Tony left the area for a minute and returned with the keys. I told Tony I wasn't driving the car today's Please, put a doubled top on the car for me. It will help keep the car dry and safe. I will be picking It up at the end of the week. I would like to personally thank you and the crew for a job well done. Please, tell the crew that drinks and food at my house Friday after work. If anyone would like to bring a friend they can bring one. I hugged Tony and we talked a little business and I gave him a check and I headed out of the shop. I jumped into my car and I headed back to the Eastside to my new room. I stopped at the deli to pick up a pastrami sandwich on rye and two sports drinks. I tasted a little of the pastrami on my way to my new room. I am going to Listen to a little R&B and jazz, Latin. The sound of Temptations, Smokey Roberson, John Coltrane, Mile Davis, Eddie Palmieri, Tito Puente, and the great Mr. Isaac Hayes. I want to enjoy the sound of joy, happiness, peace, and love and put Savannah behind me for a few hours. It is great sitting around listening to great music and enjoying the peace and tranquility of life. I knew that reality was just around the corner and the peace will soon end. I can hear the wind blowing around the window. I was having a great time but once again, I have to get to the westside. I am still looking for my mother, auntie, and Taylor killers. Moving, One place to another will only increase my will for justice.

Savannah and I are about to knock Head and only one will be standing. Who knows? She might be plotting on me. I might be the one that falls but I have a plan that is so smooth that when she coughs or sneezes I will be there with tissues and juice.

Meanwhile, I drove the car back to the westside. I parked the car. My nose started to run. My feet and hands started moving by themselves. I was having another out of body experience. I jumped from the car and let the cold winter breeze hit my face and my hands. A few minutes after the cold wind hit my face and hands my condition started to return to normal. I was able to walk quickly to my building. I opened the front door and closed it immediately behind me and I sprinted up the one flight of stairs. I turn the knob on my apartment door and the door open. I looked inside and saw Savannah sitting at the table crying and making a lot of noise. I walked by her and headed straight for the bedroom where I started taking off my clothes and prepared myself for a bath. Her crocodile tears and loud noise did not fool me one bit. I headed into the bathroom. I was saying to myself. What would be her next move? I started showering and thinking about Savannah's action in the last few weeks. I finish my shower, dry off, and then put my bathrobe on. I was standing there and everything hit me at once. Miss Savannah never came into the bathroom and I left my gun on the bed in the bedroom. I sat down on the sides of the tub and I began to think about what will be Savannah, next move. Savannah stands by the door waiting to shoot me. Savannah has the upper hand. I said to myself call her, it can't hurt. So; I started to call her name. A minute or two went by and I started calling her name again Savannah, Savannah, Savannah, This time I couldn't hear a thing. My body and mind started to shut down. I had no place to hide or run. I was saying my prayer and thanking all the people that help me along my journey of life. The knob started to turn. My six feet two-inch statue turned to three feet nine inches. My eyes began watering. I anticipated what was coming next. The door opens and in step Savannah in her bra and panties. She held nothing in her hand but her eyes were cold sharp as a knife. Savannah looked me up and down and said what all the noise about you needed my services. You did say too much when you came in and saw me crying. What is your story? I looked dumb and follow Savannah out of the bathroom throws the bedroom and into the living room. She took a seat on the sofa bed and I took a seat on the chair bed. Savannah looked over toward me and said gets your butt over here. I jumped up and I took a few steps toward Savannah and I turned and I headed into the bedroom. I took the gun out of my jacket and put it under the pillar. I grabbed the two blankets and king size quilts and headed back into the living. I place the blanket in front of the sofa bed and I place the quilt on the left-hand side of the blankets. I grab Savannah and place the quilt over us. I put my big arm around her and started to squeeze her slowly but gently. The music (stay in my corners) began to play. After, fear and mayhem two murders try to find a moment away from reality.

The next morning I reach for Savannah and she is gone. I turned over and went back to sleep. Two hours later. I got up and I took a shower and I made me three eggs over-easy and toast. It was mid-morning. I cleaned the kitchen and I took a seat at the table. I continue planning what Savannah and I will be wearing on our trip. We both want white or black corduroy pants. I want black corduroy pants with a white silk shirt and black underwear. I don't know what Colors blouses or undergarments Savannah will be picking out. We both like black. We also will be picking out our boots, Sneakers bomber jackets. I will check the internet for the stores or shops that have everything we need. I hope Savannah will be ready to go shopping today, tomorrow, or online. I continue to work on the shopping list until noon. I check around the houses, making sure all the rooms are clean, and that everything is where it should be. The bed is made floor vacuum and dishes and pans are all put away. I put my coat on. I check my gun and head out the door. I am standing in front of my building and the cold wind is blowing against my cheek. I then turn right and head toward the ABC store. I entered the ABC store and I purchased a fifth of E&J. The area was deserted. No, one was out in the street making money. I wanted to know what was going on. I made a few phone calls and people started to drift out in the cold. You know I am a social worker. I get people together to buy my goods and services. We don't force people or threaten people. We just have what consumers need. I am not a pimp or drug dealer. We make every effort to have the best product so our complaints are few and that people return again and again. I started to see my worker pass by or stop at the ABC store. I am sending out a text stating that all money owed (Baby Boy Enterprise) is to be in by five o'clock pm. Please text in your time slot. I started walking around the community stopping at grocery stores, restaurants, bodega, barbershop, and salons, restating my message. It's Mid-afternoon, I started checking my text messages and my bottle of E&J. I had fifteen text messages and a three-quarter bottle of E&J left. It was time to get upstairs and start collecting my money. I started checking the time slot my workers sent in. I have switched the times. So, workers don't run into each other. I have set my post where I want my torpedoes to be. Torpedoes are hired gunmen that help me protect (Baby Boy Enterprise). I station them on both ends of the street in cars. I also have two men downstairs in my building at the door entrance and two more men on the roof landing. All the protection is because of Savannah and her reign of terror in the community. We don't know sure if Savannah or someone else responsible for the shooting and mayhem but (Baby boy Enterprise) needs to be protected. Meanwhile, all the workers have their time slot and the money is starting to come in. I should be finished by six o'clock. The workers are moving in and out fasters I expected. I should have the money put away before Savannah returned for the evening. Everything is moving as planned. The workers are in and out and the money is safely tucked away. Savannah is not in yet and the forecast calls for cold and windy conditions. We also expect up to eight inches of snow. I move into the kitchen and prepare myself two turkey sandwiches with lettuce and tomatoes and a cup of tea. I placed my sandwiches on my plate and I picked up my cup of tea and started walking back into the living- room. All of a sudden the door opened and Savannah walked in. Her eyes were as red as hot red peppers and she was as cold as ice cubes. I helped her off with her coat. I went into the bedroom and brought out a blanket and I put it around her. I gave her my hot cup of tea and one of the sandwiches. She sat down on the sofa bed for more than half an hour before she took a sip of tea or bite of the turkey sandwich. It took another half an hour before she said what the hell is up. She stated I am as cold as an iceberg. She took another bite of the sandwich and sip on tea. She started talking. I have just walked one mile because the bus never came. My feet are a cold block of ice. I never felt this bad in my life. It is a good time to put a rope around her neck but just a few hours earlier she had the drop on me and let me walk out the bathroom. I am waiting for the right place and at the right time. I stroll back into the Kitchen and prepare Savannah another cup of tea and some chicken noodle soup. As soup and tea being prepared. I walked back into the living- room and I sat close to Savannah. She started talking and I listened. She apologizes for letting her brother use the car and now brougham is missing. She again apologizes for being so nasty and distances toward my family. She concluded by saying all I ever wanted to be is your soul mate for life.

I put my head on her lap and said (what word we use when we try to deceive). Savannah fell asleep knowing her words left me confused and speechless. The next morning I woke up and I turned over. I found Savannah still asleep in bed. I was shocked. I do remember how she came home. Her eyes were deep red, her lips were black and her speech was gone, fear and death had interred her life, and turning back was not an option. I kissed her on the cheek and said to myself that darkness has taken over both of our life. The devil has conquered both of us. I slowly ease off the bed and headed toward the bathroom but before I put my foot in the bathroom I turn around and head back to the top of the bed. I looked under the pillows and I removed my gun. I still recall the last time I left my gun on the bed while Savannah was in the house and me in the bathroom. I felt like I had lost my mind. I felt numb and confused. I was on my knees saying my prayers. I was waiting for Savannah to turn the knob and shoot me. I left nothing undone this time. I took my gun with me. I place my gun around my underwear and place it on top of the hamper. I showered and I dried myself off. and I put on my bathrobe. I put my gun in my bathrobe pocket. I turned the knob on the bathroom door and headed out the bathroom into the bedroom. I glanced over at Savannah who still seems to be sleeping. I continue walking through the bedroom into the living room and on into the kitchen. I prepare myself a cup of tea and an egg sandwich. I headed back to the living room. I sat down at the chair-bed. I began to eat my sandwich and drink my tea. I turn on the television and the radio. I looked at the television and I listened to the radio. I looked and listened and I continued seeing a red flash in my eyes. I did know what to make of it. so, I moved my head away from the flashing light but the light came into the living room and It started hitting off the wall. I placed my tea and sandwich down. I headed into the bedroom. I looked over on my side of the bed and I found out that It was my cell phone that was flashing. I checked the messages. The message stated that your son has been shot and I should get to the hospital immediately. I started putting on my cloth as fast as I could. I stopped only to pick up my tea and sandwich and I ran out the door. I did not look over at Savannah nor did I kiss her. I headed straight out the door down a flight of stairs into the street and to my car. My heart was pounding so I took a sip of tea. Help me with my out of body experiences I continued to the hospital. The snow was packed high on the side streets. Six minutes later I pulled into the hospital Emergency entrance. No parking spot. I double-parked next to a green equinox and I ran inside. The first person I saw Zoe Brown and her two brothers. The three of them give me an update on my son's condition. He has been shot three times and he is still on the operating table. My mind goes blank and my two cousins help me to a chair. Once again tragedy entered our family. Zoe asks If I needed anything. I looked up and slowly said a cup of tea. While one of the brothers goes and purchases me a cup of tea. Zoe and other brothers are by my side. A few minutes later, he returns with a cup of tea. The flavor of the tea was mint. I slowly began to sip on the tea. The tea is very hot but the flavor is awesome. After a few sips, I began to feel much better. I begin to ask questions? Where was he? Who was he with? Why was he out there at that hour? The three of them look at me with a blank stare. I slowly push myself up and out of the chair. I walk over to the waiting room and I look through the glass. I see twenty or thirty people sitting around on chairs, tables, and the floor. I am trying to see where Mary is seated so I can let her know that I am here. I look around again and find her sitting in the northeast corner. She has ten or eleven people sitting in front of her. I have to get to her without making a fuss. I open the door. I pulled my hat down near my eye and slowly inched my way toward her. All of a sudden my daughter spots me and she gives her mother a sharp elbow. Her mother jumped up and she started waving her hand backward. letting me know not to come any closer. I turned around headed back out the door. A few seconds later Mary and my daughter emerged from the waiting room. The three of us just jumped into each other's arms. After a minute or so Zoe and her two brothers join in. Then one by one-two by two-three by three they start coming out of the waiting room and join in the hug and love they all have for my son. It was very emotional. Tears started to run down my face. Mary wiped my tears and more tears came down. We were there for more than twenty minutes asking God for one more chance to be with our son. Mary lifted her head and slowly the crowds dispersed in every direction. Mary grabbed my hand and I grabbed my daughter's hand and we headed back into the waiting room and back into the northeast corner. We sat down and one by one they came by and gave us hugs and kisses and said how much they were praying for our son. The candy store man, Restaurant workers, Pizza store workers, Used cars salesman's, Drugs stores workers, even old Mr. Tim. Mr. Tim is a beggar. He carried a sign for food and money at the intersection. They are all theirs for my son and family. Time pasting, I needed to check on things. I asked Mary if I could be excused. She looked at me and said, I see you still have jokes. You go do your thing but don't leave the hospital. I made a few phone calls and got the ball rolling. I need two people to tail Savannah. Savannah was to be following everywhere she went. I want her to know that we are following her. If she has anything to do with the shooting of my son these are her last hours. Secondly, I need six torpedoes at the hospital three on the inside and three on the outside of the hospital. It's time for action. I have been playing footie with Savannah for a long time. Lastly, everyone needs to check in hourly. I need to know what is going on in the street. If you see anything that you need to take action on don't wait to call or text me take actions, call.

Meanwhile, I headed back into the waiting room area. I scan the rooms for any new faces. I see my mechanic Tony and also see a few of his worker's behind him. They are my old running buddy Bo, Mike, Stacey, and Rob, Fig. We give each other a wave. I continue moving toward Mary and my daughter but before I get there I see my brother and his wife. I also see my other brother and his wife. The showing of love and kindness by family and friends is overwhelming. Cold snow day, Tears rolling down my face. I am a few steps away from Mary when up from being seated at a tabletop pop Taylor James Sister Nina. The girl was looking fine as a picked chocolate bar. I hugged her and told her I will be calling her soon. I am sitting next to Mary and she hit me with a sharp elbow. (like in basketball) Women have good instincts. They can read your body language before you know what you want to do. I put my arm around Mary and said to myself women make you act like a fool even when trying not to look. We were sitting around the waiting room anticipating the news from the doctor. The seconds seem like minutes. The minute seemed like hours. The hours seem like days. Reality has come full circle and we are all praying, texting, thinking that the outcome would be positive. IIt'smid-afternoon, not a word has come downstairs from the doctor. I received four text messages from outside that stated no movement from Savannah. A minute or two later, I am sitting in the waiting room and A knock comes on the waiting room door. Everyone stood up as Mary, my daughter and I made our way through the crowd and into the doctor's office. The office was only large enough for two people but not for four people. We all somehow squeezed in the office. My mind went blank before the doctor started to speak but before the doctor had finished Mary and my daughter were holding me tight. I gave a thumbs up to my family and friends that were waiting. We heard the clap, whistle and cheers throw glass windows. Anticipation, waiting, stress had everyone on edge but little hope brought love and joy. We continued talking to the doctors. He gave us all his immediate opinion and update. He also said that only family members are allowed in the recovery room at this time. He will be in the recovery unit within the next two hours. The nurses are cleaning him up and getting him ready for family members. We thank the doctor for his hard work and we slowly started to rejoin the family members and friends that were there waiting in the waiting room with hugs, kisses, and prayer for us. We again thank everyone for being there for us. As family members and friends slowly start leaving the hospital. A day of tragedy and despair returns love and hope to our family. The sky was gray all day but now we can see little sunshine through the cloud.

Savannah, where could she be. She, sleeping in the apartment. Or did Savannah leave behind me early this morning? She is as cunning as a lion and as slippery as a snake. She could be outside the hospital now waiting to shoot or kill my family member or friend. No one has seen her morning or the afternoon. A few minutes later I get a text stating that Savannah was seen coming out of the police station. I don't know what is going on but we must keep our eyes and ears open. She could be a police informant or undercover officer. Either way, we are going to find out. What is She up to? Who Savannah is working for? I want everyone on her trail. I am sending four of the six torpedoes from the hospital to watch her every move and report back to me. I waited for half an hour to pass. Anticipation, Savannah's next move, I gave Savannah a call. I tell her to meet me over At (Joe's Pizza. She said ok that she will be there within the hour. I hung up and I started texting the crew to meet me over at (Joe's Pizza). Before I could push the send button I received a text reading raid at Joe's Pizza. The only person who could have sent me this text is Savannah. She is working both sides of the fence and keeping everyone in suspense and on their toes. I have to counteract what Savannah is doing. Meanwhile, I walk back to the hospital room where Mary and my daughter are keeping vigil over my son. I stop a few minutes from all the crap and mess that I am into and I check on my family members. I check to see if they need anything to eat or drink or if they need to use the restroom. I will hold my son's hand for a while and they can take time out for themselves. A few days earlier my son and I were talking about going to the football games and hanging out. Life throws you all kinds of curb and you never know when or how It will end. I sat there thinking about the day he came into the world and the day I brought him home. The peace and joy I had as sun and rainbow followed me every place I took my son. I never thought it would end. I woke up and went to sleep every day with joy and peace in my heart. Where did I go wrong? (Beginning of my end?) Remember, all the good times my son and I had together. The hours, months, and years we spent in playgrounds, parks, hiking, swimming, boating, fishing, and overnight camping. I see all the pictures clear in mind and tears start to roll down my face. I squeezed his hand a little harder and he slowly opened his eyes. A smile comes over my face and more tears fall from my eyes. I felt happy, sad almost simultaneously. I was happy because he opened his eyes. I felt sad because he was lying there and there's nothing I could do to ease the pain and hurt that he was feeling. I wanted revenge but I wanted my son to feel better now. I would give any amount of money just to see my son get up and walk out of the hospital. Yes, the mind can play tricks on you. It can give you false hope or outcome but when you have joy and faith nothing anyone can say or do can stand in your way.

It's early Friday morning and I have earnings to run. I have to wait to see what Mary scheduled. I give Mary a call. The phone rings, no answer. She is not awake yet. I called her back. I switch the smartphone over for things to do today by the hour. I pencil in (pick up car) between 11 am – 2 pm. Next, I pencil in check on (Savannah movement) all day. Next, call Tony to confirm tonight get together or reschedule another date and time. 12- 1 pm next, pick up money from the business between 5 pm 7 pm. recall Mary or my daughter 7 am-10 am Everything I needed to do today was a pencil in and I could make changes if needed. I left my son at the bedside and headed to the cafeteria for a cup of tea to unwind from night and rewind for the day. I purchased the tea and headed back to my son's room. The night nurses had come in and given him a shot to keep him sedated while he continued to mend. They also wipe his ears and face. They were finishing up as I returned to the room. I thanked the nurses for the work that they were doing and I gave each nurse a twenty-dollar bill and added that breakfast was on me. I pulled a chair close to the bed and extended my arm out to reach his hand and I squeezed his hand and he opened his eyes. My heart skips a beat and tears roll down my cheek. Suddenly, the phone rang. I checked the number it was the snake herself looking to create havoc, mayhem, and confusion. I answer the phone by saying good morning Savannah in return she said good morning and how is your son's. I stated that he was holding his own. She jumped into the conversation and said can we get together this afternoon. I said, I am very busy with my son now and I don't have any time for anything else. However, I have a few things to say to you, Miss Savannah. You have been with me through the death of my mother, aunt, best friend Taylor, and now the shooting of my son. The word on the street is that you are responsible for all three actions. So, I am asking as a friend can you remove all your belongings from the apartment. Savannah jump in, you can't kick me out. Where am I going? You can move in with your brother or mother or someone else. I am going to give you a week to get you another place and remove your things out of my apartment. The phone went silent. Savannah came back on and said I am three months pregnant and I am having your baby. I am not moving out because of your insecurity. I have nothing to do with your mother, aunt, friend, and son. All I want you to do is to come home. I can assure you that whatever problem that is between us we can work it out. I could not listen to any more smooth talk so I hung up the phone. Savannah has once again turned around everything that I had planned to do. Who is this woman? Who is she working for? I need to find out a little more about Savannah. So I started back to where we first met. I met her in the park watching a little league hardball game during the summer month. She was with two other young women. All three ladies were carrying a purse across their shoulders. I didn't know what was going on but I can look back and see that all three could have been young policewomen. I was in the park's watch my young team participate in the first playoff game. I was cheering and watching the young boys play defense. It was the first time I saw the team after buying the uniforms in early spring. I didn't know the team was that good? I smiled as the ladies came into the park and sat next to me. I was surprised at first but the ladies all look great. Savannah sat next to me and I started up a conversation right away. I remember asking her for her number and would she like to attend a barbeque that weekend. She said yes and things started moving quickly from there. We date twice a week. We attended sporting events, movies, social events, and parties. I can't say if people were following us taking pictures or had listening devices but being out in the open all avenues were possible. We continued to grow closer and within six or seven months Savannah moved in with me. Savannah never talks about what she did or where she went. She would leave early in the morning and return midafternoon or early evening. Savannah had secrets but she kept them to herself. I never question her. I have secreted also and mum was the word. I know now that communication should have been better and we might not be in such a love-hate relationship today. Our two years together have been nothing but great. However, Savannah has a split personality. Savannah is one person in the early morning and another person in the late evening. I don't know what she is doing to trigger these tantrums. I don't know what I can do to help her. Savannah would get up early morning making noises. You could hear the water running in the kitchen and the bathroom. You could hear the radio and tv. You could also hear chairs being dragged from one room to another. It sounded like three or four people in the house. I tried to talk to Savannah about the noise of singing, banging but went in one ear and it came out of the other. The evening Savannah was the complete opposite. She would come home make dinner, She would make sure that whatever I needed was at my fingers tip. She was warm and kind. She did everything to make the evening enjoyable. Once in our relationship, I met Savannah's mother. I hope never to see her again. She is the lowest of the lowest person. One day she said to me if my daughter isn't satisfying you. I will take her role anytime. My ears mind rungs with level hate, disapproval. I gave her a scowling look and I turned my back on her. I never hated a person much as I did her mother at that very moment. What would make her mother stoop so low? I didn't want Savannah to see the hate I had for her mother. So, I retained a smile on my face and I held her hands. I didn't want to show any disrespect because I was in her momma home. I wanted to run out of the door. I can still see her eyes all over my body. The hate for her mother followed me back to my apartment. I tried saying a few words with Savannah about the conversion I had with her mother as we rode back home. I can recall that Savannah was as non concerned, dish detergent. Her eyes said talk about something else. I saw that Savannah and her mother had an unusual relationship. They use sign language to communicate with each other. Both of them could talk and speak well. What were they trying to hide? I don't know and I did not care what the two of them were up to. I know now that one of them or both of them may be up to something. I am the one who is going to put this puzzle together.

I am still at the hospital holding my son's hands. I squeeze his hands once and I watch him open his eyes. I am so confused by all the mess and mayhem. I don't know one end from another. I have to tie all the knots together and unravel them one by one. I pulled out my smartphone and started to text two of my partners. I ask them to check around and see if anyone saw Savannah, Savannah's mother, or brother around any of the shooting of my mother and aunt or Son or Taylor James. (Please do not text any information back to me) Please bring in all information when turning in your package. I have started the ball whirling. I am going to sit back and watch come in.

Meanwhile, The nurses came into the room and they began checking on my sons. They wipe down his face, ears and neck and they check all the equipment that is hooked up to him. I see a few minutes to step out the room and get me another cup of tea and toast. I walk out the room and down the hall to the cafeteria. I pay for tea, toast and apple. I started walking back towards my son's room. I get a little closer to the room and I see the nurses moving around at a top pace. Blue light comes on. The door and the curtains to windows close. I am looking at the door. I am holding my tea and toast, apple with no one to talk to, and no place to go. A few minutes pass but it seems like hours. The door opened and the nurses started to walk out the room. The last nurse touched me on the shoulder and she said that he is stable now you can go in. I feel a little uneasy so I take a deep breath. I slowly walk into the room and look over at the bed and my son looks like he is just sleeping. His eyes are closed and he little smiles on his face. I put the tea and toast down and I pulled a chair close to the bed. I don't reach for his hands this time. I began singing an old song (I trust you) It's a good thing to be free and doesn't let pain and hurt get you down. I was sitting there singing about the good things that life may offer. I looked up and my son's mother walked into the room. I was a little startled, but very happy to see her. She was looking good and she dressed to make your eyes move. Mary was wearing a long blue bomber coat and long blue cotton dress and long blue one -inch heels boots. I said good morning I don't know why I left you for someone else. You know it was under my breath. Mary moved a little closer and she started talking about all the phone calls this morning. Why did I have to leave so early? Why didn't I want to spend more time with my son? She talked on and on. I looked up at her with a half smile and said I just wanted to know where you were and if everything was all right. She bent over gave me a kiss and said I know you and I know what you want. I ended the small talk and started talking about how the night went. I let her know that our son had a small set back but the nurses were on top of their game every step of the way they assured me that he was stable and that I needed to rest easy. Mary gave me a hug and she thanks me for being there with our son. She continued to chat and said, I know you have some things that you have to do so you run along and get back to your girlfriend. I will see you around. I assured her that I had a few more hours to spare and If she did not have breakfast. I would go to the cafeteria and get something for her to eat. I got up and I took my cold tea and toast and I tossed it in the trash can. I walk down the hall to the cafeteria. I ordered two eggs, sandwiches with tea and coffee and 2 fruit cups. I paid for my order and headed back to my son's room. I pulled up another chair to the side of the bed and handed Mary her breakfast. I then sat down and we both began to eat. Mary was looking so good that I started to nip smaller pieces of my sandwich just to feel her nearness. I started undressing Mary with my eyes. lust was running through my mind like water. I got up and headed to bath- room to check if there was a lock on the door. There was no lock on the door but the bathroom door had a dead- lock sliding lock on the inside of the bathroom door. I peep out the door in the direction where Mary was sitting. I almost bit my lip looking at her. She was Finnish up her sandwich and began to sip her coffee. I dash over to where she was sitting. I grabbed her hand and off to the bathroom we went. I locked the door and I put my tongue down her throat and started easing off my pants. Mary ease off her pants also. I moved over to the toilet seats where I sat down. Mary moved over close to me and straddle herself on top of me. We began to make love. We started holding each other tighter and tighter and moving up and down. We were sweating like two people in basketball game round one was over, Mary and I were pushing for round two I stood up from the toilet seat and Mary lock her legs around my waist We started over again This time we began making a lot of noise I move over to the toilet and gave It a flush. The flush helped to drown out some of the noise but Mary and I were into deep passion. We took about thirty minute returns our son's bedside. I looked at Mary and said what have I got myself into. Savannah the mother of my baby to be and Mary the mother of my two young adult children's. It's (the Beginning of my end) I didn't go straight back to my son's bedside but I walked out in the hallway and made a few calls. I called Tony, my repair-person and I informed him that I will not be picking up my remodel brougham this afternoon. Secondly I will not be hosting the party tonight. I also thank him for the use of the car and I will still be using the car. He thanked me for my update and he added if anything else he could do please don't hesitate to call. I thank him and I hung up the phone. I waited a few minute than I call my number two man and I inform him that I will be leaving the hospital within the hour but, before, I reentered my son hospital room. (I had a flash- back of all the mayhem and mishap that lead me to where I am today.) It started when Zoe knocked on my door and informed me that my mother and aunt were murdered. A few days later Zoe, Charles, Carrel and I got together. We joined up for a evening of fun adventure. The evening turned out to be a night to remember. We heard bullets flying and siren blaring but we saw no injuries. The same night we headed up the street to an after- hour club's to buys something to eat. We get in the elevator and before we push the buttons for the floor. We look through the small window on the elevator and we see a man and a woman fighting. The womens is swinging a knife wildly. The man knocks the women's down but before he can do anything she is back up and swinging the knife again. The man is bleeding all over the lobby. We push our floor and continue on to our destination.Later, Savannah is sitting next to a police car and the diagram of a body is outlined on the street. My car is missing. A week later we grab Savannah, brother and take him to my Aunt houses where he mysteriously disappeared. We are on our way back home from my Aunt house. I received a text from Taylor, sister. I learned that she was killed a few days ago. That same week, I received early morning text and I learned that my son had been shot). I returned back from my flash back and found reality staring me in the face. I looked through the hospital windows and I watched people coming and going bundle in large coats, scars, hats and gloves. I could hear the wind blowing as I stared through the window. I turned left and took the five steps back to my son's room. I look in and I see his mother holding his hands. I grab a chair and I pull it close to the bed. I placed my hands on the top of Mary, hands. My son's eyes slowly started to open. I whispered to him assuring him that we will be there every step of the way until you can walk again. I looked over at Mary bent over and I gave her a kiss. I told her it was time to go. I grab my hat, coat and scarf and walk slowly out the room. The long walks down the hallway seem cold and lonely. I am out the door and the cold and wind seem like relief from all the turmoil. I am in the car and I am heading back home for more unrest, uncertainty. I am driving as fast as the light changes. I hear the cold wind hit the car from every side but the heat from the car helps to keep me warm. I am turning into my block looking for a parking spot. I find a parking space three or four buildings away. I get out of the car but instead of heading into my building I turn into the first building I come to. I ascend the stairs to the roof. I cross over the roof and head to my building. I descend the stairs but as I get closer to my apartment. I begin to hear voices. I can't place the voice but I continue down the stairs. I hear a door close and then I hear someone exit the building. I am in front of my apartment door. I put the key in the lock and open the door. I walked in and I closed the door behind me. I head straight to the bedroom. I see Savannah coming out of the bathroom. We give each other a kiss. Savannah asks are you hungry. I say yes and she continues out the bedroom, I take my gun out my pocket and place it in my bathrobe. I continue taking off my clothes and head toward the bathroom with my bathrobe across my shoulder. I leave the bathroom door open. I place my bathrobe across the shower curtains with my gun pocket facing inside the tub. I hear Savannah voices, but I can't make out what she is saying. I finish up my shower grab my bathrobe and some clean clothes. I sit on the end of the bed and I put on my clean clothes. I lay across the bed. A few minutes later Savannah enters the bedroom with Breakfast. The plate contains hotcake, sausages, eggs and orange cut in four pieces. I smiled and gave Savannah a big kiss. Savannah leaves the room. She returned with a tub of water. She place It in front of me and she placed my feet in the water. Was this my end? I continue to eat with one hand on my gun and two eyes on Savannah. I finish eating and Savannah clears the plate. I pulled out my computer and waited for Savannah to reenter the room. Savannah reenters the room with a big smile on her face. She saw the computer and she asked what the hell was up. I pulled her close to me and said to her time to order our matching outfits for our weekend trip. We need Hats, coats, paints, boots, shirts, socks and underwear. Savannah checked out the stores and outlet and recheck the store and outlet until she completed everything we needed. She stated that all the clothes will be at our residents within two working days. Savannah closed the computer place under the bed. She leaped on me like snake hunting prey. She did give me a chance to react or say anything. Savannah pulled off my tee shirt and shorts. She pulled off her gown. She throws everything on the floor. We moved a little closer to each other. Savannah makes a noise and the love making was on. I put one arm around her and with the other hand I took two fingers and put it in her mouth Savannah was bucking like the she wasn't going to ever stop but I slowed her down almost to stop but Savannah got some wind from within and I had to hold on with both hand smiling and calling her name sweat was pouring from our body. Savannah couldn't stop bucking, A little noise came from her and she began to slowed down little than little more than she came to stop We gave each other a kiss and savannah roll over I easy my way out the bed grab my underwear and headed to bathroom I wash up but Savannah never join me in the bathroom I rejoin her by bed but Savannah was still in the same spot I left her in. I tried to move her with one hand but I couldn't move her. I used both hands and I moved her just little. Urine was all in the bed. I moved her a little more and all her body fluids had come down. I did know what to make of it but Savannah had died after having sex. All I could do is call my best friend and tell him what had happened. I also called Zoe Brown and told her to get over here quickly. The two came over, they checked my apartment from top to bottom and they removed all the guns and money from the apartment forty five minute had elapsed since she had died. I called the police. My best friend left but Zoe stayed with me. The police came and I told them what had happened but they wanted more informants. I explained to them that I don't use drugs but I do love wine and liquor. I don't know what Savannah uses beside alcohol. You can check her purse or pockets. They asked if anything else I would like to add to this investigation. I said no. The paramedic arrived and checked Savannah vital signs and they declared her deceased. The paramedic stated they could not move her until the corner arrived. A few minutes after the paramedic left the police specialists arrived. They began to take pictures of everything in the bed- room and the bathroom. They checked the bathrooms and bedrooms from top to bottom. They picked up hair samples, rug samples around Savannah on bed and on the floor. They also took hair samples from the bathroom. I was in a tail- spin between my son and Savannah. I did not know what was going on. The police stop talking to me. Zoe and I left the apartment and headed to the roof of the apartment. I needed air and I needed someone to vent to. Before, We stepped on the top landing. Zoe yells out to me. you forgot to call her mother. I stopped in my tracks and I stared at the brick wall on the top landing. I looked over at Zoe and asked her could call for me. She moved close to me and said, I call for you but everything you love is slowly being taken away from you. I could only listen. I didn't know what was happening. Zoe made the call. I open the roof door and the cold wind slap me in the face. Zoe joined me on the rooftop and put her arm around me. Tears started falling from my eyes. Zoe looked, smiled and said you are human. I look back at Zoe and say uncertainty has followed me since I left my aunt home. What is my fate? Zoe changes the subject, She stated that Savannah mother wishes for me to call her now. I said I will call her in a few minutes. Zoe headed back down to the apartment but I stayed up on the roof until I was cold from head to toe. I didn't want to see or hear anything. Finally, I open the roof door and descend to my apartment. Zoe met me coming down the last few steps. She grabbed my hand and led me into the apartment and to the kitchen where she made me a cup of hot tea. I sat in the kitchen with my hat and coat on while drinking the tea. I finished my tea and I placed my cup in the sink. My phone started to ring. It was my kid's mother. She asks me what the hell was going on over there. The phone went silent for a moment. I began to speak. I inform Mary that Savannah had died and that they were waiting on the corner. Mary stated did you kill her. I said no but the police have to rule me out of their investigation. Mary hung up the phone. Mary is upset. Savannah is dead and my son is in the hospital with three gunshot wounds. Savannah, mother is on her way to my apartment. I need all my strength to continue, Throught. next day, weeks and months. Zoe and I waited in the kitchen anticipating the knock from Savannah mother. Zoe has been my rock through everything. I couldn't have asked for a cooler cousin to be around. The police specialist are starting to pack their bags and exit the apartment but they leave behind one officer to stay with the body and wait on the corner. Zoe moves away from the table and she checks the refrigerator and cupboard. She was looking for food to start making soup. Zoe found a few items she started making the soup. The aroma from the soup started spreading throughout the apartment. The aroma from the soup gave me a warm feeling inside despite the cold weather outside and Savannah lying dead in the bedroom. We are still waiting, Savannah mother to arrive. I sat at the table listening to the news and weather. An hour and half had passed and Zoe soup was ready. The aroma from soup had passed into the hallway. I got up from the table and I retrieved two bowls from the cupboard and placed them on the stove next to Zoe. I asked the police officer if he enjoys a bowl of soup. He said yes and I retrieved another bowl and place It on the stove. Zoe fixes the bowls of soup. She hand delivered it to me and the police officer. We began to eat and all of a sudden three big knocks on the door. I jumped up from the table and headed to the door. I opened the door. Savannah mother, standing there. She took her hand and tried to move me to the side. I told her not to do that again and to take both hands out of her pocket. I also inform her that a police officer was in the apartment and if you do anything stupid he would lock your ass up. She became friendly and polite as she walked around the apartments. She sat down and waited for us to finish our soup. We finish the soup and I gather up the bowls. I wash them and put them into the dish drain. I walked out the kitchen and found Zoe and Savannah mother in the bedroom looking at Savannah. I did not go in but stood at the doorway. I watched Savannah mother stroke her hair and say a prayer for her. She slowly walked out the room. She passed by me in the doorway and I started a conversation with her. I stated that Savannah and I were to take a trip this weekend and that we purchased matching outfits. If you would like to have her outfit or would you like me to return the outfit and buy Savannah a dress for the funeral. I also asked her if she would like to ride with Zoe and myself to purchase a casket for Savannah. She said yes, so, Three of us put on our hats, coats, scars, and gloves and spoke briefly to the officer before leaving the apartment. I walked ahead and I warmed up the car while Zoe and Savannah's mother stood in the lobby entrance. A few minutes later I pulled up in front of the building and Savannah's mother sat in the front seat and Zoe sat in the back seats. We are on our way to Ike funeral Home. It is the local funeral home in the area. Everything we need for Savannah's funeral burial should be at the funeral home. We arrived at the funeral home. We went inside meet with Mr. Day. He is the funeral director. We walk into his office and he gets the lady coffee and me tea. He pulled out a book with the different colors and styles of caskets. He hands the book to me but I pass It over to Savannah, mother. She browses the pages until she sees the casket she wants. She passed the book to me and Zoe and I looked at her choice. We both agreed to her choice. The price was over fifteen thousand dollars. Zoe looked at me and Savannah, mother stared us down. She was trying to intimidate the two of us. I stood up and stared back at her but Zoe intervened and she said to me. It was not a time to argue with her. let's just purchase the casket and move on to the store for the dress. You know that your son needs you. I don't need you going to jail for this crazy lady. I was mad as hell but I said ok. I thank Mr. Day for his time and told him that I would like to purchase number 1752 in white with silver trim. He informed us that the casket will be here in two days and that we needed seven thousand dollars down payment. I headed to the car to get the money while Savannah, mother signed the paperwork. Zoe looks on and she signs under Savannah, mother. I return with the money and check the papers work and I sign under Zoe names. Mr. Day thanks us and stated that the funeral will be held on Friday at 11 30 am Savannah, mother started her shit again. She tells him, Mr. Day, The funeral will not be held at the funeral home but at the Christ Day Church where she was baptized. Mr. Day said no problem we will call the church and ask them what time they would like to start. Savannah's mother said ok and we shook hands with Mr. Day. The three of us walked out the doors. The next stop is the dress shops. We can get shoes and dresses for Savannah. I looked for a black and white dress and white shoes. I ask Savannah's mother if the color is ok. She just looks at me. Zoe and I found the dress we were looking for. We showed the dress to Savannah's mother and she said I don't like the color. I want a light blue dress for my daughter. I said ok and we started to look for a light blue dress Disgusted, piss-off, The way Savannah mother is treating us. I stopped shopping and I headed out of the store. I leave Zoe with the money and head for my car. I am sitting in my car-mad as hell because of the way Savannah's mother has been treating us. I left because I didn't want a big argument in the store. She has been against everything we were doing from the very start. I wanted some way to get on the same page with her but everything we did Savannah, mother turned it around. The hate and miss trust I had for Savannah's mother was too much for me to handle. My hand started to move by Itself. I looked out the window and saw a little shop where I could buy a cup of tea. I opened the car door and headed across the street. I stumble just before I step on the curb. I hit my head on the sidewalk. I was lying there between two parked cars. My head was bleeding and I couldn't call out for help. I was lying there thinking about my son in the hospital. Will I ever see my son again? Will I be able to attend Savannah's funeral? Will Zoe come out of the store and find me. Will I ever get to drive my white on white brougham? Everything seems to be moving faster and faster as I slowly slip away. I could only feel the cold wind hitting my face. I never got the chance to find my mother or aunt killer. Savannah kept me distracted and I couldn't see past my nose. Days came and went and Savannah was always the topic of conversation. I could not turn things around. Murder, lust, money was all I ever thought about. So, I lie here today with no place to go and no one to turn to. What will they say at my funeral? Who will attend? Who will write my obituary? Everything I did for people, friends, and family and I find myself lying in the gutter lonely and forgotten. (the beginning of my end)

Printed in the United States
By Bookmasters